Inside the NFL

THE
ST. LOUIS
RAMS

BOB ITALIA
ABDO & Daughters

Published by Abdo & Daughters, 4940 Viking Drive, Suite 622, Edina, Minnesota 55435.

Copyright © 1996 by Abdo Consulting Group, Inc., Pentagon Tower, P.O. Box 36036, Minneapolis, Minnesota 55435 USA. International copyrights reserved in all countries. No part of this book may be reproduced in any form without written permission from the publisher.

Printed in the United States.

Cover Photo credits: Wide World Photos/ Allsport
Interior Photo credits: Wide World Photos

Edited by Kal Gronvall

Library of Congress Cataloging-in-Publication Data

Italia, Bob, 1955—
        The St. Louis Rams / Bob Italia.
                p.   cm. -- (Inside the NFL)
        Includes index.
        Summary: Provides an overview of the history and key personalities associated with the team that joined the National Football League in 1937 as the Cleveland Rams, played in Los Angeles, before moving to St. Louis in 1995.
        ISBN 1-56239-541-6
        1. St. Louis Rams (Football team)--History--Juvenile literature. 2. National Football League--History--Juvenile literature. [1. St. Louis Rams (Football team)--History.] I. Title. II. Series:
        Italia, Bob, 1995— Inside the NFL.
        GV956.S85I83   1996
        796.332'64'0977866--dc20   95-43595
                                                                              CIP
                                                                              AC

CONTENTS

The Old New Team

In 1995, the Rams played their first season in St. Louis. But the Rams were not a new team. They had been in the National Football League (NFL) since 1937—first in Cleveland, then in Los Angeles. Despite all those years, the team has yet to claim a Super Bowl title.

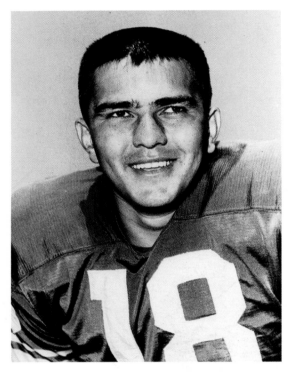

Los Angeles Rams quarterback Roman Gabriel, 1963.

The Rams have had many star players on their roster. There were quarterbacks Bob Waterfield, Norm Van Brocklin, and Roman Gabriel. The Rams also had the "Fearsome Foursome" defensive line of Rosey Grier, Merlin Olsen, Deacon Jones, and Lamar Lundy. And there was Eric Dickerson, one of the most exciting running backs who ever played the game.

The St. Louis Rams have a new cast of players, led by quarterback Chris Miller. Isaac Bruce has already established himself as one of the league's best wide receivers, and the Rams overall play has been inspiring. But it is too early to tell whether or not the St. Louis version of the Rams will ever break the franchise's Super Bowl drought.

**Opposite page:
Running back Jerome Bettis.**

From Cleveland to L.A.

In 1937, the Cleveland Rams entered the NFL. Between 1937 and 1944, the team posted a 25-49-2 record without a single winning season. Even worse, they finished last twice.

Because of their failure to win, football fans in Cleveland did not support their team. So Rams' owner Dan Reeves looked for another city to call home. Before the 1945 season, Reeves decided Los Angeles was the place to be. But the Rams spent one more year in Cleveland. It was a year the team turned its fortune around—thanks to their new quarterback, Bob Waterfield.

Waterfield starred at UCLA before signing with Cleveland in 1945. In his first season, Waterfield became Cleveland's starting quarterback. Immediately, the Rams started winning.

With a winning team in their city, football fans began to pack Municipal Stadium to watch Waterfield. On the strength of his accurate passing, the Rams climbed into first place. But Waterfield got hurt late in the season and was not expected to play against second-place Detroit in a game the Rams needed to claim their first division title.

But Waterfield did play—and play well. Throwing often to Elroy "Crazy Legs" Hirsch, Waterfield led the Rams to a 28-21 victory. Cleveland was the Western Division champion. Now it would host the Eastern Division champion Washington Redskins in the NFL title game.

On the day of the championship game, the temperature was well below freezing. The weather did not bother Waterfield. He did it all—ran, passed, and punted—as the Cleveland Rams won their first NFL title, 15-14. The fans went wild for their team, but it was too little, too late. Reeves soon announced the Rams were moving to Los Angeles.

Elroy "Crazy Legs" Hirsch catches the ball against the Packers, 1951.

The Los Angeles Rams

With Waterfield at quarterback, the Los Angeles Rams became one of the highest-scoring teams in the NFL. Fans still loved to watch their exciting play. Able to score points in bunches, Los Angeles was never out of a game. They proved this point in 1948.

In a regular-season game against Philadelphia, the Rams fell behind the Eagles 28-0. Finally, the offense woke up. Waterfield picked apart the Eagles defense, as he threw long passes to Hirsch and rookie Tom Fears. The Rams scored four touchdowns and earned a 28-28 tie.

In another game, the Green Bay Packers raced to a 28-6 lead. Then Waterfield engineered three touchdown drives. A field goal gave Los Angeles a 30-28 victory.

Waterfield led the Rams to Western Division titles in 1949 and 1950. But each year, Los Angeles lost the league title—first to the Eagles, then the Cleveland Browns. The 1950 title game was played in Cleveland. Los Angeles took a 28-27 lead late in the game. But Cleveland's Lou Groza kicked the game-winning field goal.

Opposite page:
Elroy Hirsch goes for the end zone against the 49ers.

Division Champs

In 1951, the Rams added quarterback Norm Van Brocklin to their offense. If Waterfield couldn't move the offense, Van Brocklin took control. The quarterback tandem often worked well.

Running back Dick Hoerner blasts through the Bears line for a touchdown, 1950.

The Rams also had an outstanding running game, led by Tank Younger, Dick Hoerner, and Vitamin T. Smith. Los Angeles averaged nearly 33 points a game as they won the Western Division title for the third straight year.

In the title game, Los Angeles faced the Cleveland Browns. Waterfield led the Rams to a 14-10 advantage. But the Browns rallied to tie the game 17-17. When the Rams offense stalled, Van Brocklin replaced Waterfield. With three minutes left in the game, Van Brocklin connected with Fears on a 73-yard touchdown pass. Los Angeles won 24-17.

In 1952, the Rams tied Detroit for first place, but the Lions defeated Los Angeles in the playoffs. In 1953, the once-happy quarterback tandem turned into a major headache for new coach Hamp Pool. Some players wanted Waterfield to be the starting quarterback. Others wanted Van Brocklin to start. After the season, Waterfield ended the dispute by retiring.

Opposite page:
Quarterback Norm Van Brocklin.

The Quarterback Shuffle

Van Brocklin did not get to enjoy his status as starting quarterback. Soon, Bill Wade joined the team and shared playing time with Van Brocklin. The new quarterback tandem soon became another headache—for players and fans. If Van Brocklin started, the fans wanted Wade in the game. If Wade started, Van Brocklin became the fans' choice.

Soon Van Brocklin got tired of the quarterback shuffle. Like Waterfield before him, Van Brocklin retired. Then he agreed on a trade to Philadelphia.

But Van Brocklin's departure did not solve the Rams' quarterback problems. Whomever started, there was always a backup waiting to get into the game. Los Angeles never got consistent play from any of their starting quarterbacks. They needed someone they could rely upon game after game.

While the quarterback controversy raged on, the Rams began to slip in the standings. Though they won the division title in 1955, they tied for second in 1958. Then from 1958 to 1965, Los Angeles failed to record a winning season. It was time for a change.

Reeves tried different head coaches. Even Waterfield coached for two seasons. Nothing seemed to work.

Roman Gabriel

During their playoff drought, the Rams continued their hunt for a consistent quarterback. From 1962 to 1964, Los Angeles used their first pick in the college draft to take a quarterback. First they drafted North Carolina State quarterback Roman Gabriel. The following year, the Rams chose Oregon State quarterback Terry Baker. Then Los Angeles used its top choice to take Utah State quarterback Bill Munson. Now the Rams had three talented but inexperienced quarterbacks. Team officials hoped that one would develop into a star.

Quarterback Roman Gabriel working out before the game against the Packers, 1967.

To make sure the Rams developed their young quarterback trio properly, they hired George Allen as head coach in 1966. But Allen, like his predecessors, used all three quarterbacks during the season, waiting to see if one true leader would emerge.

Gabriel got tired of alternating with other quarterbacks. After the 1966 season was over, he planned to go to another team. Allen spoke with Gabriel and promised to make him the starting quarterback while giving him time to develop his skills. It did not take long for Gabriel to assert himself as a star.

The Fearsome Foursome

In 1967, Gabriel led the Rams to an impressive 11-1-2 record as Los Angeles finished first in the division. Gabriel threw often to wide receiver Jack Snow, while halfback Dick Bass led the Rams' running game.

**Roman Gabriel scrambles
to pass against the Vikings.**

On defense, Los Angeles had developed one of the best defensive lines in NFL history. The line was known as "The Fearsome Foursome"—Rosey Grier, Merlin Olsen, Deacon Jones, and Lamar Lundy.

With an explosive offense and powerful defense, the Rams expected to win the NFL championship. But in the first round of the playoffs, they lost to the Green Bay Packers, the eventual Super Bowl champions. Still, the Rams had become one of the best in the NFL, and big things were expected in the years to come.

In 1969, the Rams won their division with an 11-3 record. Gabriel threw 24 touchdown passes and was named the NFL's Most Valuable Player. But once again, the Rams had difficulty in the playoffs. In the first round, Minnesota defeated Los Angeles 23-20.

Chuck Knox

Gabriel continued to lead the Rams for the next three years. But Los Angeles failed to make the playoffs. The San Francisco 49ers had taken over as the top team in the division as they won three straight Western Division titles. Once again, the Rams felt it was time for a change.

In 1973, Chuck Knox became the new head coach. Gabriel was traded to Philadelphia, and the team started winning again. From 1973 through 1979, the Rams won the Western Division title.

Knox built his first-place teams around a defense anchored by defensive end Jack Youngblood and linebacker Jack Reynolds. On offense, running backs Lawrence McCutcheon and Cullen Bryant sliced through defenses, thanks to a great offensive line that starred guard Dennis Harrah and tackle Jackie Slater. McCutcheon gained more than 6,000 yards in seven seasons, eventually becoming the team's all-time leading rusher.

Jack Youngblood (85) causes a fumble against the Cowboys.

The Super Bowl At Last

Despite all their division titles, critics considered the Rams failures because of their lack of success in the playoffs. They had never made it to the Super Bowl—until 1979.

That year, the Rams fielded one of their "weaker" teams. They finished with a 9-7 record under second-year coach Ray Malavasi and barely made the playoffs. It was Los Angeles' worst record since 1972, when they posted a 6-7-1 mark.

Something happened to the Rams in the playoffs. They transformed themselves from an average team into an unbeatable one. Despite playing on the road, the Rams won two playoff games and advanced to the Super Bowl. Quarterback Vince Ferragamo led the way.

In the Super Bowl against the mighty Pittsburgh Steelers, the Rams took a 19-18 lead. But the Steelers defense finally asserted itself and shut out the Rams the rest of the way. Pittsburgh went on to win 32-19.

No one knew what to expect in 1980. Would the Rams get better and return to the Super Bowl, or was the 1979 season just a fluke. The Rams silenced their critics by making the playoffs again. This time, they were eliminated before they could reach the championship game. After that playoff appearance, the Rams went into a tailspin. Unable to halt the losing streak, Malavasi was fired.

Robinson and Dickerson

To stop the bleeding, the Rams hired John Robinson as head coach in 1983. Robinson had achieved much success at the University of Southern California (USC), where he built his teams around a great running attack. Robinson's first goal was to sign a great running back for Los Angeles.

The Rams had the second pick in the first round of the NFL draft. Robinson could choose any college running back in the country. But he already knew who he wanted: Eric Dickerson from Southern Methodist University.

Robinson had known Dickerson since 1978. While at USC, Robinson tried to recruit Dickerson, who was a high school star in Texas. Dickerson wanted to play for USC, but it was too far from home. Now Robinson had a second chance. This time, he got his man.

Dickerson proved to be the great running back Robinson thought he would be. In his rookie year, the smooth, swift running back led the NFL in rushing with 1,808 yards in 390 carries. It was the most yards ever gained by a first-year running back—and one of the best rushing seasons ever. Dickerson led the Rams to a 9-7 record and a playoff berth. But the Washington Redskins revived an old Ram tradition, knocking them from the playoffs in the first round.

Dickerson was no flash in the pan. He was the heart and soul of the Rams offense as he led the NFL in rushing in 1983, 1984, and 1986. In 1984, Dickerson also set an NFL record for the most rushing yards (2,105) in a season. Jack Youngblood and safety Nolan Cromwell starred on defense. But the Rams lacked a quarterback who could take the pressure off Dickerson and lead them to the championship. Robinson knew his team needed a reliable passing attack if it was going to make the Super Bowl.

ST. LOUIS RAMS

Receiver Elroy "Crazy Legs" Hirsch, 1951.

30   40

Quarterback Roman Gabriel, 1963.

ST. L
RA

Quarterback Norm Van Brocklin, 1951.

20   30   40

40

10

Linebacker Jack
Youngblood, 1979.

OUIS
MS

Wide receiver Isaac Bruce
and the Rams move to St.
Louis in 1995.

40

10

Running back Eric Dickerson
joins the Rams in 1983.

ST. LOUIS
RAMS

Jim Everett

The Rams had not had a consistent quarterback since Roman Gabriel. John Hadl, Joe Namath, James Harris, Pat Haden, Vince Ferragamo, Jeff Rutledge, Dan Pastorini, Bert Jones, Jeff Kemp, Dieter Brock, and Steve Dils all tried to fill his shoes. But no one had much success. Hadl, Namath, Pastorini, and Jones had seen their best days with other NFL teams. Brock came from the less talented Canadian Football League.

In 1986, the Rams took a chance on quarterback Jim Everett from Purdue University. To help Everett develop his skills, Robinson hired Ernie Zampese as offensive coordinator. While with the San Diego Chargers, Zampese had designed a great passing game for quarterback Dan Fouts.

Everett became the starter in 1987. But his first few seasons were difficult. As a result, the Rams struggled. Even worse, Dickerson wasn't part of the offense. He held out for more money—and eventually demanded a trade.

During the 1987 season, the Rams sent Dickerson to the Indianapolis Colts for several draft choices. Now Everett was the key to the offense. He worked hard to learn Zampese's system. By the end of the year, the passing attack started clicking, giving fans hope for the following season.

In 1988, Everett blossomed into a star. He led the NFL with 31 touchdown passes—many to veteran wide receiver Henry Ellard. Running back Greg Bell also played well. He finished third in the NFC in rushing.

In 1989, the Rams improvement continued. Everett led Los Angeles all the way to the NFC title game, where they lost to the San Francisco 49ers.

Quarterback Jim Everett scrambles from a defender.

Running back Eric Dickerson.

Everett, Ellard, and Willie "Flipper" Anderson had changed the focus of the Rams offense from the running game to the passing game. Bell, Cleveland Gary and Gaston Green still ran the ball with effectiveness.

On defense, linebackers Kevin Greene and Fred Strickland, cornerback Jerry Gray, and safety Vince Newsome began to shine. Mike Lansford was one of the best placekickers in the NFL. It seemed as though the Rams were headed in the right direction as the new decade approached.

But in 1990, the Rams took a nose-dive after making the playoffs in six of the past seven seasons. Injuries and holdouts helped contribute to the shocking and disappointing 5-11 record. Everett threw for nearly 4,000 yards but was not very sharp as he also threw 17 interceptions and completed only 307 passes in 554 attempts. Kevin Greene and his 13 sacks was the only bright spot.

It didn't get any better in 1991 as the Rams started 3-3 but then lost the rest of their games for a 3-13 record. Everett continued his slide as he threw 20 interceptions and was the 14th ranked passer in the league. When the season was over, Robinson was gone. Chuck Knox took over one more time.

The coaching change seemed to wake Everett up. He threw for 3,323 yards and 22 touchdowns. Cleveland Gary rushed for 1,125 yards and had a team-high 52 receptions. But the Rams defense ranked last in the league and they finished with a disappointing 6-10 record.

Rookie running back Jerome Bettis proved to be the surprise of the 1993 season as he rushed for 1,429 yards, second in the league. It was the seventh-highest total ever for an NFL rookie. For his efforts, Bettis was named the NFL's Offensive Rookie of the Year. But Everett slumped again and battled with T.J. Rubley for the starting quarterback job. The Rams had yet another disappointing season, finishing 5-11.

The 1994 season was another disaster for the Los Angeles Rams. They won their first game 14-12 over the Arizona Cardinals, but by Week 8 they were 3-5. They would win only one more game the rest of the way and finish 4-12, good for last place in the NFC West. It was time for a change. But this time, management did more than simply look for a player who could give the team a fresh start. The Rams decided to move to St. Louis.

Receiver Isaac Bruce was the bright spot of the St. Louis offense.

The St. Louis Rams

In 1995, the St. Louis Rams got off to a magical start. They hired a new head coach, Rich Brooks, then put together an impressive winning streak.

In Week 1, Alexander Wright's leaping 30-yard touchdown catch with 3:02 left in the third quarter snapped a 7-7 tie and the St. Louis Rams went on to defeat the Green Bay Packers, 17-14.

Chris Miller lofted a pass into the end zone for Wright, who ran between two defenders and made a leaping catch in the end zone to give the Rams a 14-7 lead. Wright was signed as a free agent in the off-season. The touchdown to Wright capped an 8-play, 75-yard drive.

The following week, St. Louis beat the New Orleans Saints 17-13. In Week 3, Anthony Parker returned a fumble 28 yards for a touchdown and Torin Dorn scored on a 24-yard interception return as St. Louis spoiled the Carolina Panthers home opener with a 31-10 rout. At 3-0, the Rams were off to their best start since 1989, when they won their first five games.

The Rams extended their record to 4-0 the following week with a home victory over the Chicago Bears. In their next game, however, the Indianapolis Colts handed the Rams their first loss, 21-18.

In the game, Indianapolis forced St. Louis into its first three turnovers of the season and beat the Rams for the first time since 1971. Miller completed 26-of-45 passes for 326 yards with 2 touchdowns and 2 interceptions. Isaac Bruce had 8 receptions for 181 yards and both scores. Miller and Bruce hooked up for a 34-yard touchdown and the 2-point conversion with 52 seconds remaining to lift the Rams within 21-18, but Brian Stablein of the Colts recovered the onside kickoff and the Colts ran out the clock.

The Rams had a bye in Week 6. But the next week, St. Louis played on a Thursday night against Atlanta. Isaac Bruce established career-highs with 10 catches for 191 yards, including a pair of touchdowns, to lead St. Louis to a 21-19 victory over the Falcons— and into sole possession of first-place in the NFC West. The 191 yards were an NFL season-high for a receiver. Bruce, a second round pick in the 1994 draft, caught scoring passes of 59 and 9 yards. The 5-1 Rams moved one-half game ahead of 4-1 San Francisco, against whom they would play the following week.

Chris Miller passed for more than 300 yards for the 11th time in his career. He completed 27-of-38 passes for 328 yards and 2 touchdowns with 1 interception.

In the first place showdown with the 49ers, Elvis Grbac filled in for the injured Steve Young and passed for two touchdowns in his first NFL start and linebacker Ken Norton returned two interceptions for scores to lead San Francisco to a 44-10 rout of the Rams.

The 49ers intercepted Miller four times. Miller was intercepted only three times in St. Louis' first six games. The win moved San Francisco to 5-2 and into a three-way first-place tie with St. Louis and Atlanta in the NFC West.

Things would only get worse the next week against Philadelphia. Eagles' quarterback Rodney Peete threw a 33-yard touchdown pass to Calvin Williams and Kevin Johnson returned a fumble for a touchdown as the 5-3 Rams lost 20-9. The Rams had now dropped three out of four since their 4-0 start.

In Week 10, the Rams (5-4) suffered their third straight loss—a 19-10 defeat to the New Orleans Saints— and fell out of a first-place tie with Atlanta and San Francisco in the NFC West.

The only bright spot was Bruce, who recorded his fifth straight 100-yard receiving game to tie a club record set by Elroy "Crazy Legs" Hirsch in 1951. Bruce had eight catches for 135 yards, including a 55-yard touchdown. He led the NFL with 1,073 receiving yards.

§

Though the Rams were sputtering into the second half of the season after a great first-half start, St. Louis fans had plenty of reasons to cheer. Not only was the NFL back in their city, they had an up-and-coming team to watch. Isaac Bruce was rapidly becoming one of the best wide receivers in the NFL. And Chris Miller proved he could get the ball often to his talented teammate. With more steady play from Miller and the defense, the Rams could become a playoff contender.

GLOSSARY

ALL-PRO—A player who is voted to the Pro Bowl.

BACKFIELD—Players whose position is behind the line of scrimmage.

CORNERBACK—Either of two defensive halfbacks stationed a short distance behind the linebackers and relatively near the sidelines.

DEFENSIVE END—A defensive player who plays on the end of the line and often next to the defensive tackle.

DEFENSIVE TACKLE—A defensive player who plays on the line and between the guard and end.

ELIGIBLE—A player who is qualified to be voted into the Hall of Fame.

END ZONE—The area on either end of a football field where players score touchdowns.

EXTRA POINT—The additional one-point score added after a player makes a touchdown. Teams earn extra points if the placekicker kicks the ball through the uprights of the goalpost, or if an offensive player crosses the goal line with the football before being tackled.

FIELD GOAL—A three-point score awarded when a placekicker kicks the ball through the uprights of the goalpost.

FULLBACK—An offensive player who often lines up farthest behind the front line.

FUMBLE—When a player loses control of the football.

GUARD—An offensive lineman who plays between the tackles and center.

GROUND GAME—The running game.

HALFBACK—An offensive player whose position is behind the line of scrimmage.

HALFTIME—The time period between the second and third quarters of a football game.

INTERCEPTION—When a defensive player catches a pass from an offensive player.

KICK RETURNER—An offensive player who returns kickoffs.

LINEBACKER—A defensive player whose position is behind the line of scrimmage.

LINEMAN—An offensive or defensive player who plays on the line of scrimmage.

PASS—To throw the ball.

PASS RECEIVER—An offensive player who runs pass routes and catches passes.

PLACEKICKER—An offensive player who kicks extra points and field goals. The placekicker also kicks the ball from a tee to the opponent after his team has scored.

PLAYOFFS—The postseason games played amongst the division winners and wild card teams which determines the Super Bowl champion.

PRO BOWL—The postseason All-Star game which showcases the NFL's best players.

PUNT—To kick the ball to the opponent.

QUARTER—One of four 15-minute time periods that makes up a football game.

QUARTERBACK—The backfield player who usually calls the signals for the plays.

REGULAR SEASON—The games played after the preseason and before the playoffs.

ROOKIE—A first-year player.

RUNNING BACK—A backfield player who usually runs with the ball.

RUSH—To run with the football.

SACK—To tackle the quarterback behind the line of scrimmage.

SAFETY—A defensive back who plays behind the linemen and linebackers. Also, two points awarded for tackling an offensive player in his own end zone when he's carrying the ball.

SPECIAL TEAMS—Squads of football players that perform special tasks (for example, kickoff team and punt-return team).

SPONSOR—A person or company that finances a football team.

SUPER BOWL—The NFL Championship game played between the AFC champion and the NFC champion.

T FORMATION—An offensive formation in which the fullback lines up behind the center and quarterback with one halfback stationed on each side of the fullback.

TACKLE—An offensive or defensive lineman who plays between the ends and the guards.

TAILBACK—The offensive back farthest from the line of scrimmage.

TIGHT END—An offensive lineman who is stationed next to the tackles, and who usually blocks or catches passes.

TOUCHDOWN—When one team crosses the goal line of the other team's end zone. A touchdown is worth six points.

TURNOVER—To turn the ball over to an opponent either by a fumble, an interception, or on downs.

UNDERDOG—The team that is picked to lose the game.

WIDE RECEIVER—An offensive player who is stationed relatively close to the sidelines and who usually catches passes.

WILD CARD—A team that makes the playoffs without winning its division.

ZONE PASS DEFENSE—A pass defense method where defensive backs defend a certain area of the playing field rather than individual pass receivers.

INDEX